DATE DUE

DEMCO 38-296

For my parents   SA
For Louisa   AA

Text copyright © 1994 by Susan Akass
Illustrations copyright © 1994 by Alex Ayliffe

Published by Caroline House
Boyds Mills Press, Inc.
A Highlights Company
815 Church Street, Honesdale, PA 18431

Printed in Singapore

Publisher Cataloging-in-Publication Data
Akass, Susan.
Swim, number nine duckling / story by Susan Akass ; pictures by Alex Ayliffe.
–1st American ed.
[32]p. : col. ill. ; cm.
First published 1994 by ABC, All Books for Children, a division of
The All Children's Company Ltd., London.
Summary : A little duck who's afraid of the water goes for his first swim
and learns there was nothing to fear after all.
ISBN 1-56397-421-5
1. Ducks–Fiction–Juvenile literature. 2. Fear–Fiction–Juvenile literature.
[1. Ducks–Fiction. 2. Fear.] I. Ayliffe, Alex, ill. II. Title.
[E] 1995 CIP
Library of Congress Catalog Card Number 94-71349

The text in this book is set in 16-point Cheltenham.
The illustrations are done in torn paper.
Distributed by St. Martin's Press

10 9 8 7 6 5 4 3 2 1

Swim, Number Nine Duckling

Story by SUSAN AKASS
Pictures by ALEX AYLIFFE

Boyds Mills Press

Delushka Duck waddled through the farmyard with her nine newly hatched ducklings behind her.

"My ducklings must learn how to swim," she said to herself as she headed for the pond.

Number Nine was at the end of the line. He was the smallest, and he had to run to keep up.

Delushka led them past the cows and under the
fence. She stopped by the reeds and called out, "Numbers!"
"One!" "Two!" "Three!" "Four!" "Five!" "Six!" "Seven!"
"Eight!" "...Nine!" gasped Number
Nine as he scurried to catch up.
"Excellent!" said Delushka.
"Swimming is easy—just
follow me."

She pushed through the reeds and
there was the pond. Number Nine did not
like the look of it. "Line up and in
you go," called Delushka
as she plunged in.

Squeaking with excitement, the ducklings lined up.
Delushka counted as they splashed into the water.
"One, Two, Three, Four, Five, Six, Seven,
Eight... Come on, Number Nine!"

Number Nine shook his head.
"Don't worry, you'll float," Delushka
promised. "All ducks float."

Number Nine felt the water with one small foot.
"It's cold," he said.
"It doesn't feel cold when you're in," his mother promised.
"It's deep," he said. "I don't like it!"
"All ducks like water!" exclaimed Delushka.
"I don't!" said Number Nine, stepping back.
Delushka sighed. "He'll
join us when he sees
we're having fun,"
she thought.

But Number Nine did not join them. He sat on the bank, wondering what to do. A large black beetle climbed a reed beside him.

"Why aren't you swimming?" asked the beetle.

"I don't like water," answered Number Nine firmly.

"Neither do I!" said the beetle. "Who wants to get wet? I stay dry by climbing tall reeds. You should try it."

"All right," said Number Nine. He jumped up and placed one foot on the bottom of the reed. It bent flat.

"Help!" shouted the beetle.

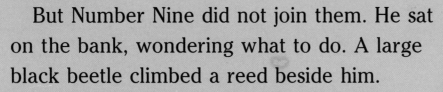

Number Nine took his foot off the reed.
It sprang up and catapulted the beetle
over the pond.

"Silly idea!" muttered Number
Nine. "Ducklings don't
climb reeds."

A dragonfly hovered above Number Nine's head.

"Why are you sitting there?"

"I don't want to go swimming," scowled Number Nine.

"Try flying," called the dragonfly. "It's more fun."

Number Nine flapped and flapped his downy wings, but without feathers, he couldn't fly.

"Poor little you!"
said the dragonfly.
And off she flew,
twisting and turning,
swooping and gliding.
"Show-off!" cheeped
Number Nine. "Ducklings don't fly."

"Why so worried?" croaked a small frog.
"I can't swim," replied Number Nine.

"Try leaping across the
lily pads instead," said the frog.

Number Nine leaped.
But he landed in exactly
the same place.
"Keep trying!"
laughed the frog, leapfrogging
over Number Nine's head.
"Ducklings don't leap," muttered
Number Nine crossly.

Delushka swam over.

"Who have you been talking to?" she asked.

"A beetle, a dragonfly, and a frog," replied Number Nine.

"And what have they told you?"

"Silly things, like how I should try climbing or flying or leaping. Ducklings don't do things like that."

"Oh," said Delushka. "What do ducklings do?" Number Nine thought for a moment. Then he said, "They follow their mother ... and ... they swim."

"Come along, then," said Delushka gently. "Let's swim."

Number Nine took a deep breath and in he went. His mother was right. It didn't feel cold at all! He bobbed up and down on the water.

He paddled his feet, and he skimmed
across the surface. "I can swim!" he squeaked.
"Time to eat!" called Delushka.

The ducklings swam to the other side of the pond, hungry after their swimming lesson.

"We will hunt for food in the long grass," said Delushka. She waddled through the grass with her head near the ground, and the ducklings copied her.

Number Nine didn't know what he was searching for. Then something wiggled in front of his beak, and he squeaked with alarm.

"It's a worm, Number Nine! Eat it!" called Delushka.
But Number Nine did not like the look of it.
"Eat it? I can't eat that."